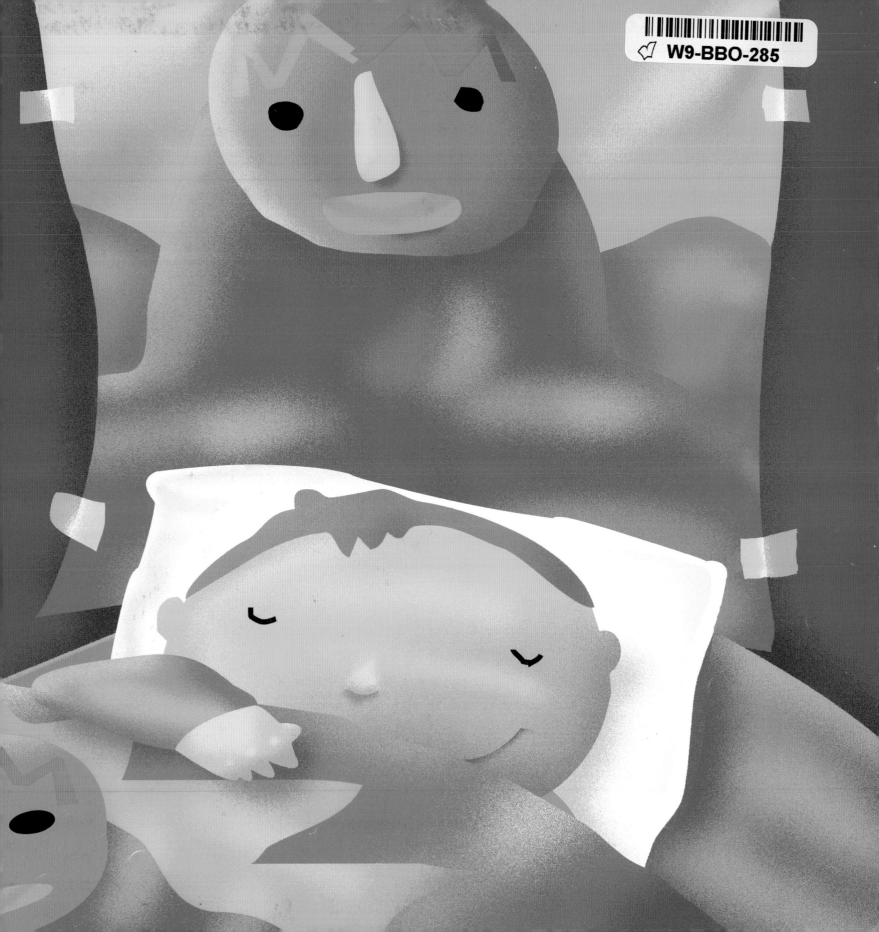

TRICYCLE PRESS
a little division of
Ten Speed Press
P.O. Box 7123
Berkeley, California 94707
www.tenspeed.com

Book design by Tasha Hall
Typeset in Frutiger
Illustrations rendered on an Apple
computer Power Macintosh G4
using Adobe Photoshop v.6.0

Library of Congress
Cataloging-in-Publication Data
Harrison, Kenny, 1954-
    How I became champion of the
        universe / by Kenny Harrison.
        p. cm.
    Summary: A little wrestling fan
is surprised to become the new
champion of the universe after he
uses his secret weapon.
    ISBN 1-58246-077-9
    [1. Wrestling—Fiction.] I. Title.
PZ7.H2525 Ho 2002
[E]—dc21   2001008034

First printing, 2002
Manufactured in China
1 2 3 4 5 6 7 — 06 05 04 03 02

To my wife, Michelle,
for your unwavering
love and support,
and to Rachel and
Max—my champions!
(thanks . . . Wesley!)

HOW I BECAME CHAMPION OF THE UNIVERSE

by
Kenny Harrison

Tricycle Press
Berkeley • Toronto

I love wrestling.
I wrestle all
the time.

I wrestle my big sister.

I wrestle my best friend.

Wrestling my dad is the most fun of all.
I always win, because I have a
SECRET WEAPON.

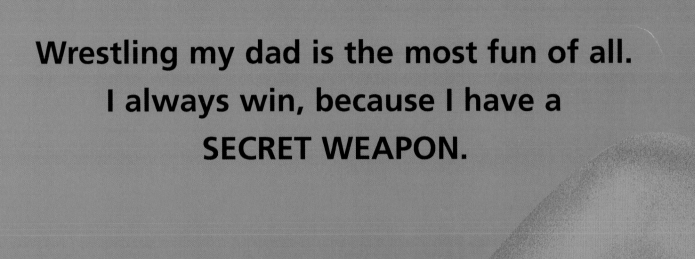

When I'm really good, Mom lets me watch Mighty Max. He's my favorite wrestler. He's champion of the world!

One day a challenge was sent from deep in outer space...

SUPER DUPER
ENTERTAINMENT
EXTRAVAGANZA

ATOM SMASHER
FROM PLANET Z

VS

MIGHTY MAX

FOR THE
CHAMPIONSHIP OF THE
UNIVERSE!

And Dad got us tickets!

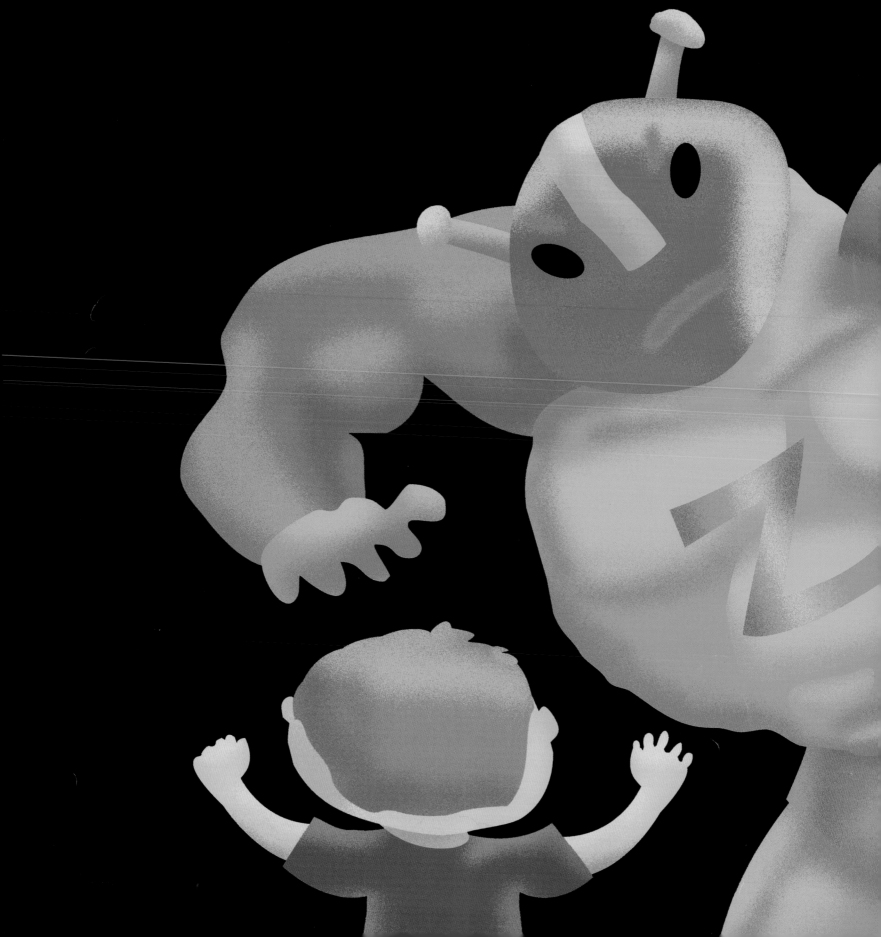

The next thing I knew I had Atom Smasher
right where I wanted him.

Time to use my secret weapon.

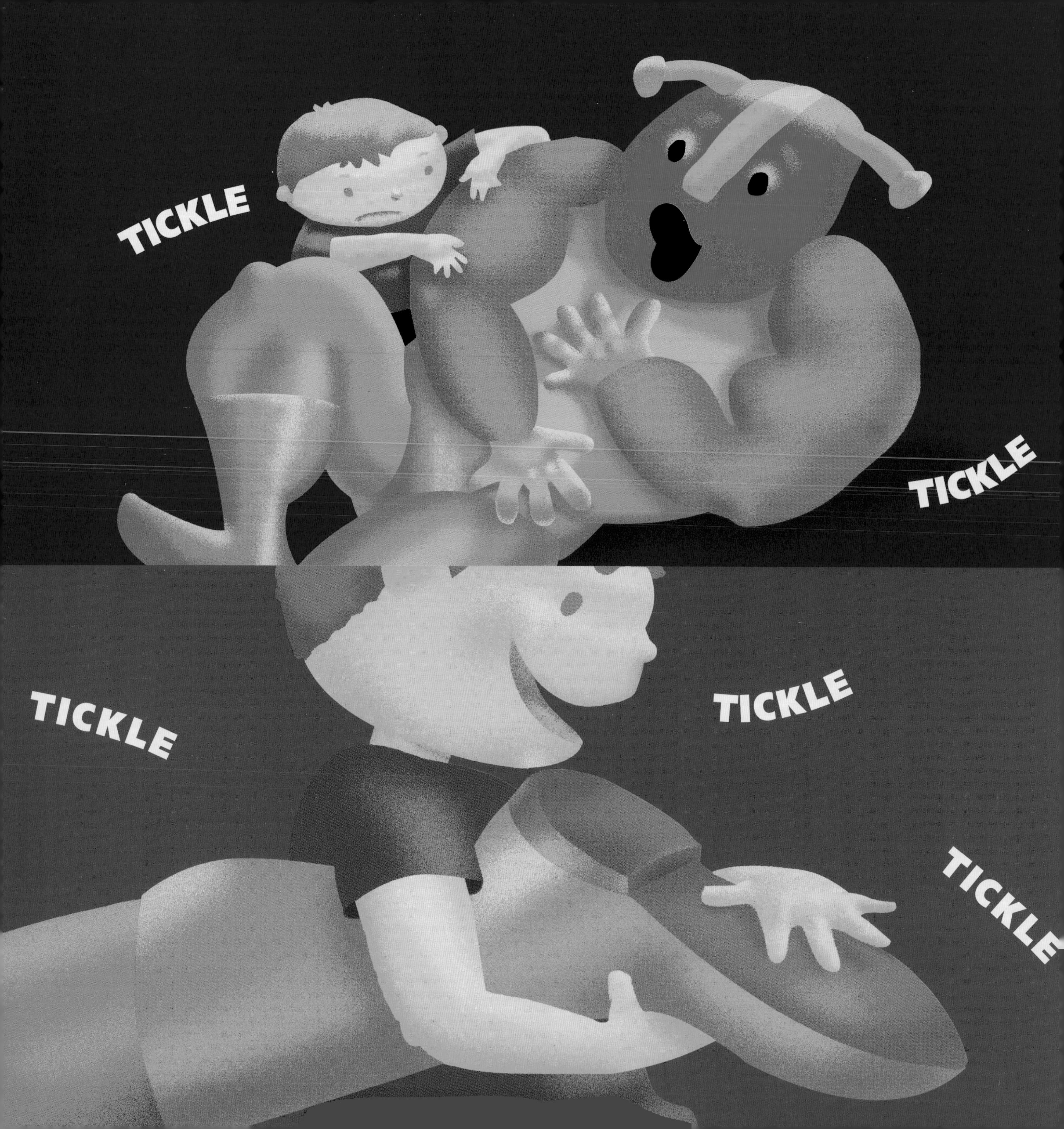
TICKLE
TICKLE
TICKLE
TICKLE
TICKLE

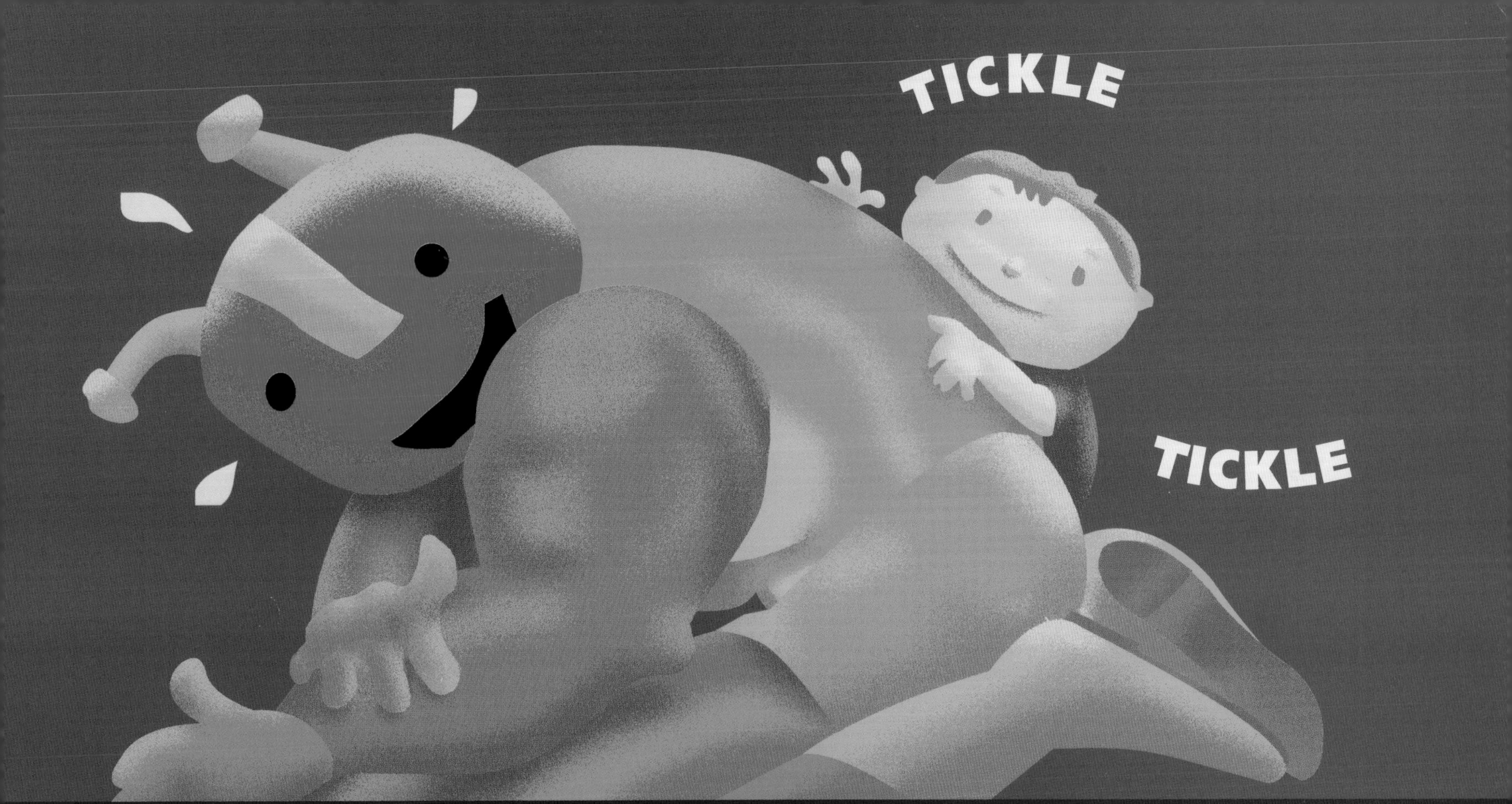
TICKLE
TICKLE

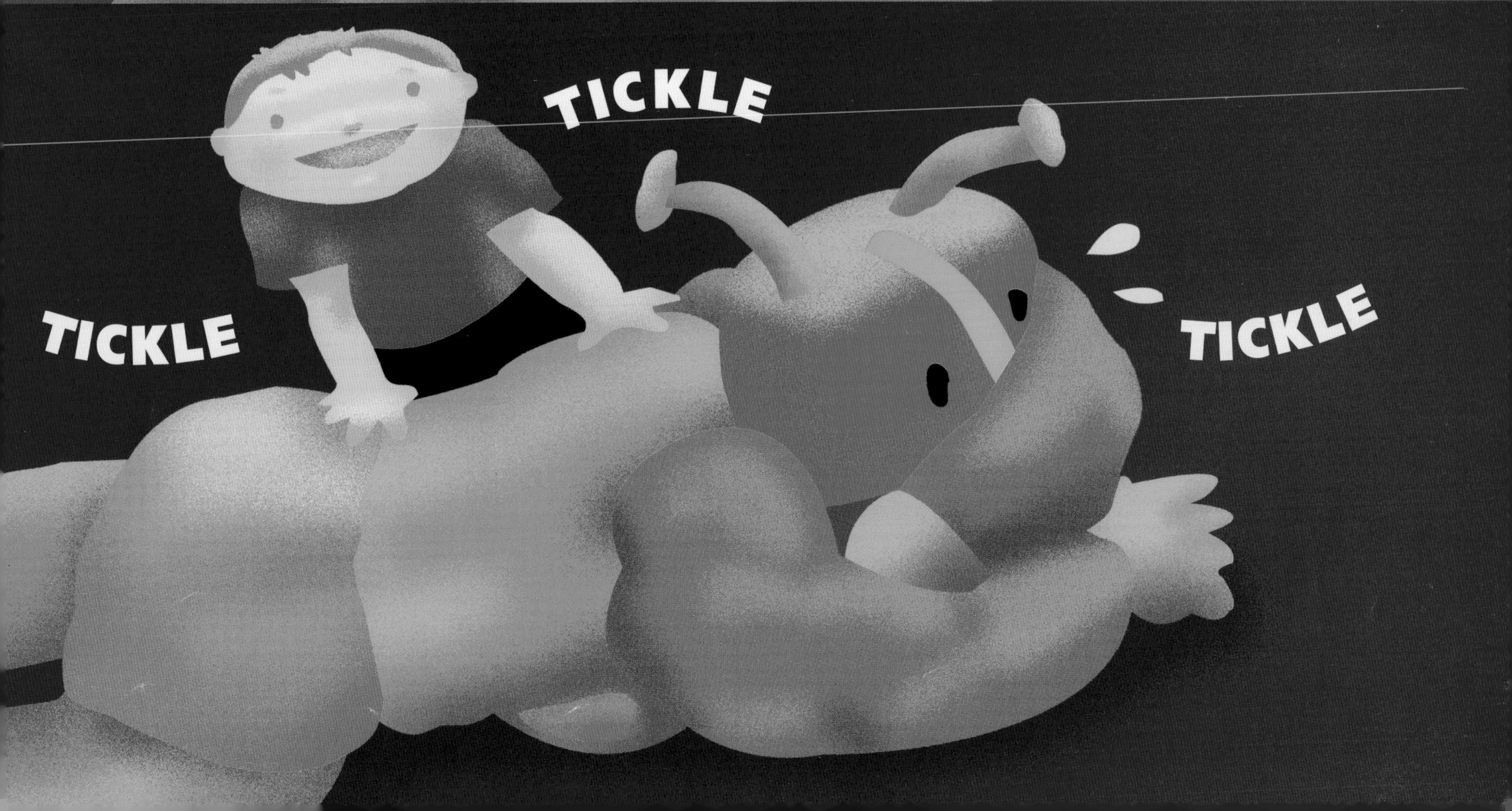
TICKLE
TICKLE
TICKLE

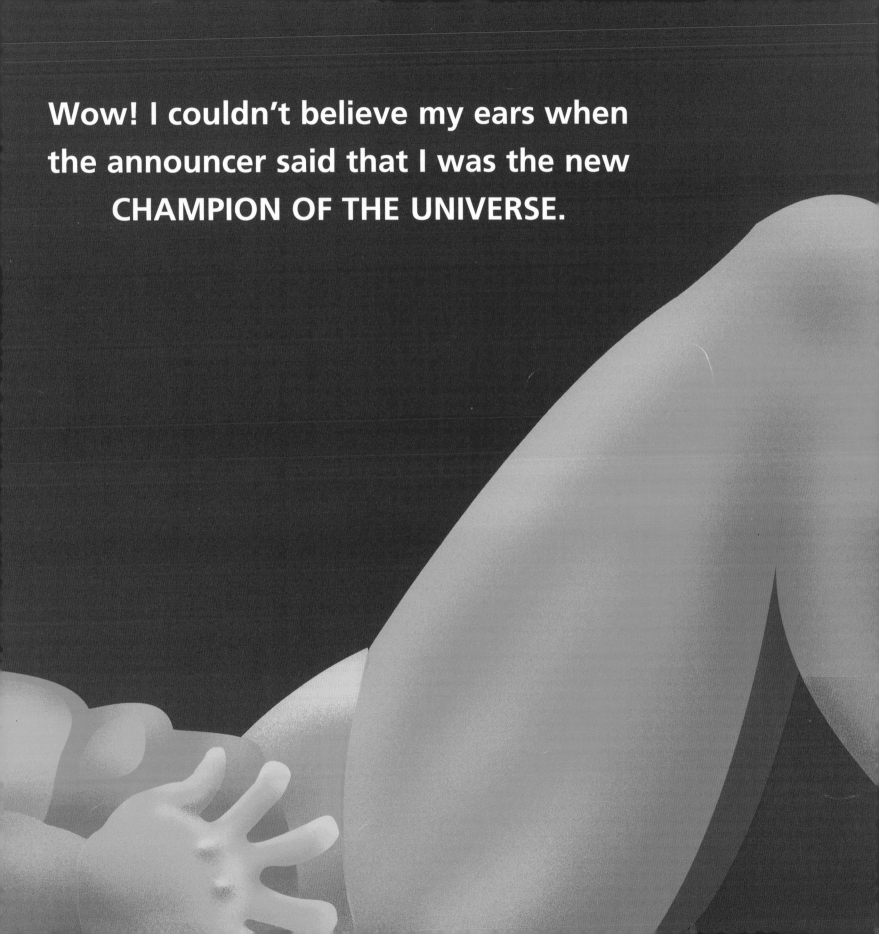

Wow! I couldn't believe my ears when the announcer said that I was the new CHAMPION OF THE UNIVERSE.

THE CROWD WENT WILD!

Now I have this great belt

CHAMPION OF THE UNIVERSE

I get to wear whenever I want.

CHAMPION OF THE UNIVERSE

f I can only get it away from my sister.
Time to use my secret weapon!

TICKLE
TICKLE
TICKLE
TICKLE
TICKLE

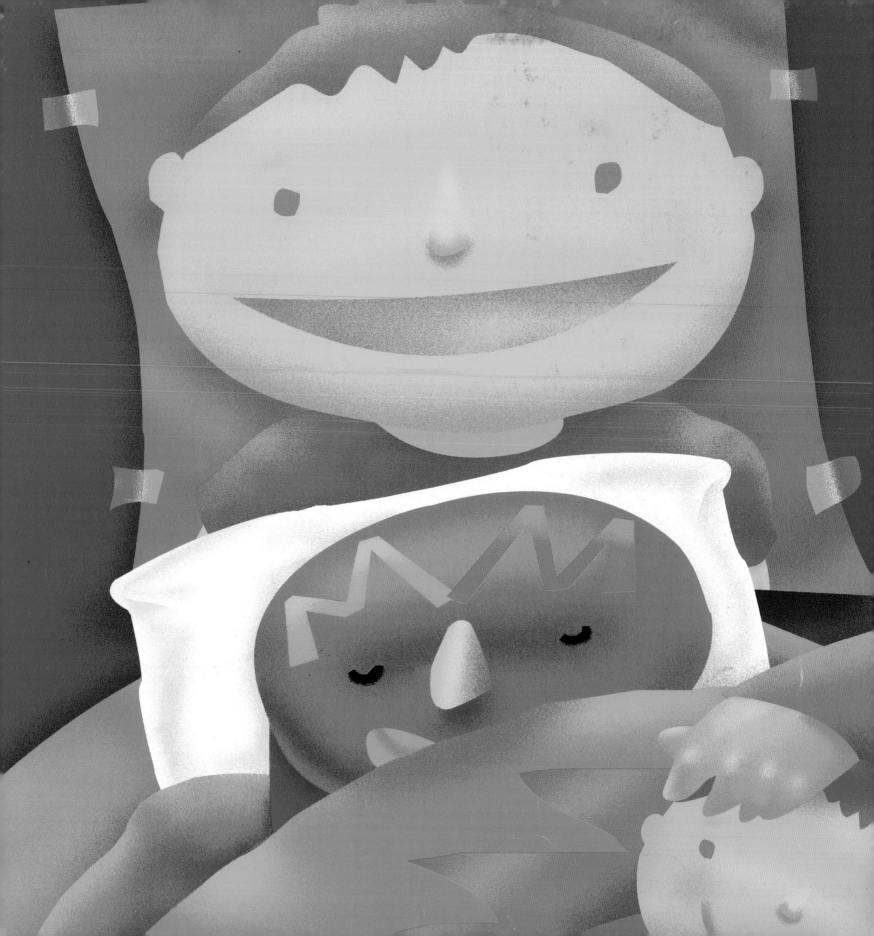